SPLASH of Flash Animation

My sincere thanks to Michele Frolla, from Next Digital, Melbourne, for allowing her story to be told and for designing this book.

Dear Reader

Join Michele Frolla, a talented Flash animation designer, as she creates the most exciting-looking animation for Internet pages!

AT SCHOOL, I LOVED CREATING AND DESIGNING COLOURFUL, AND INTERESTING PROJECTS.

MICHELE FROLLA

Few women work in Flash animation advertising, so we are lucky to meet one of them in this book.

I hope you enjoy reading about Michele and her job in Flash animation advertising as much as I enjoyed writing about her story for this book.

Sharon Parsons

Contents

SPLASH of Flash Animation

Pages 20–21
TEXT TYPE
Exposition

1 A Flash Animation Designer

Meet **Michele** Frolla

Michele Frolla is a Flash animation designer.

Flash animation makes things move or flash on websites. It is used in advertisements.

Michele works for an advertising company in Melbourne, Australia. Her job is to design Flash advertisements for websites.

Michele at work

Languages

Michele: an Italian Name

Michele is an Italian boy's name. Michele Frolla was named after her Italian grandfather. To make it a female name, change it from Michele to Michela.

the Italian flag

Italy

What Makes Michele a Good Flash Animation Designer?

Michele is a very good Flash animation designer. She:

- can think of new, fun ideas quickly
- has excellent computer-design skills
- can design Flash animation advertisements that look exciting.

Michele talks to a client. She tells them her ideas for a new Flash advertisement.

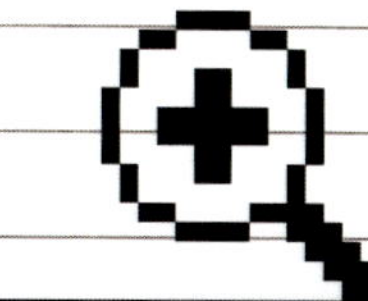

The Author **Interviews** Michele

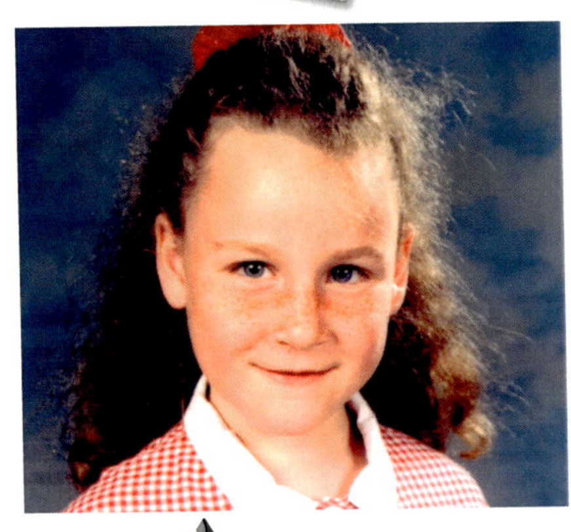

Michele in Grade 3

After I thanked Michele Frolla for her time, I asked her many questions.

A Primary School Question:

Did you enjoy creating and designing at school?

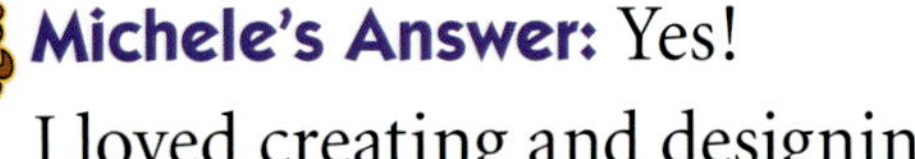

Michele's Answer: Yes! I loved creating and designing colourful and interesting projects for my teachers.

A Computer Question:

When did you become interested in computers?

Michele's Answer: At primary school. In the 1990s, computers were new. I loved them and I wanted to find out how they worked.

A First Flash Animation Question:

When did you create your first Flash animation?

Michele's Answer: I created my first Flash animation at secondary school. It was easy!

A Flash Animation Question:
What did you create in Flash?

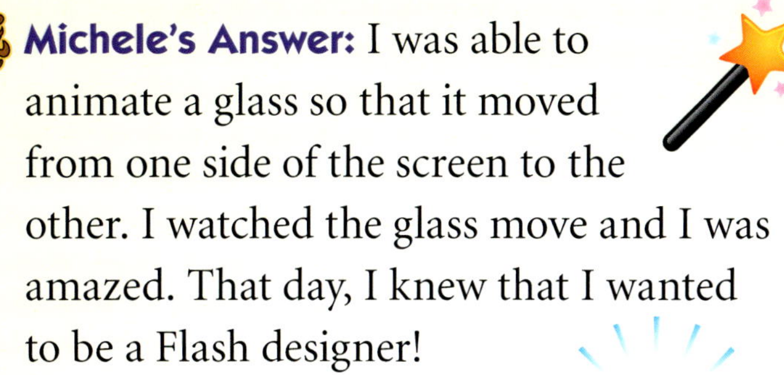

Michele's Answer: I was able to animate a glass so that it moved from one side of the screen to the other. I watched the glass move and I was amazed. That day, I knew that I wanted to be a Flash designer!

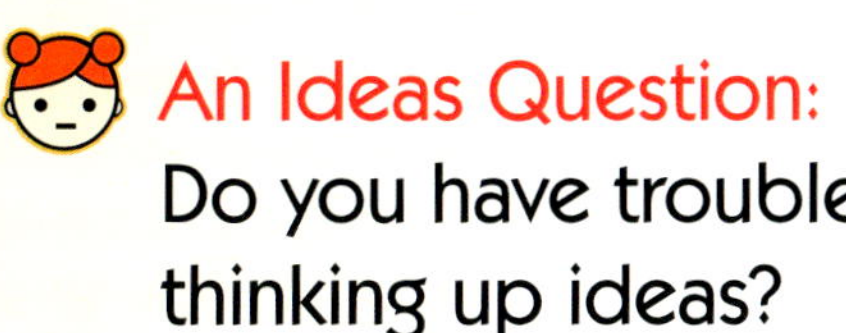

An Ideas Question:
Do you have trouble thinking up ideas?

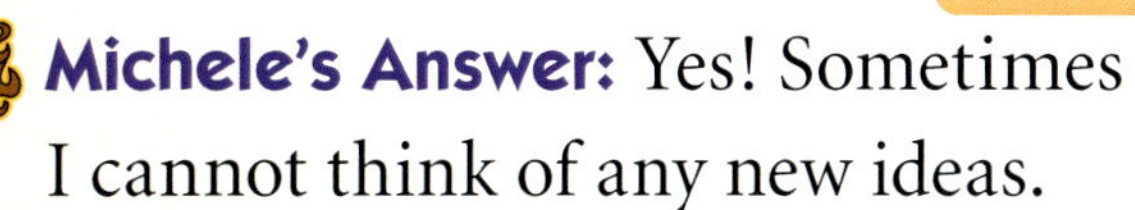

Michele's Answer: Yes! Sometimes I cannot think of any new ideas.

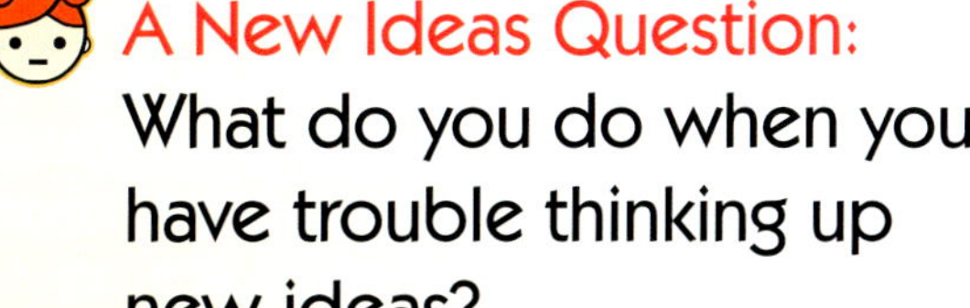

A New Ideas Question:
What do you do when you have trouble thinking up new ideas?

Michele's Answer: I don't panic. I look at magazines and "surf" the Internet for ideas. I don't use other people's ideas, they just help me think of my own Flash animation ideas.

A Work Question:
How much time do you spend working with Flash software?

Michele's Answer: About 20% of my working time is spent in Flash.

A Challenge Question:
What's a big challenge in Flash animation design?

Michele's Answer: Designing tiny advertisements to fit down the side or in a corner of a web page.

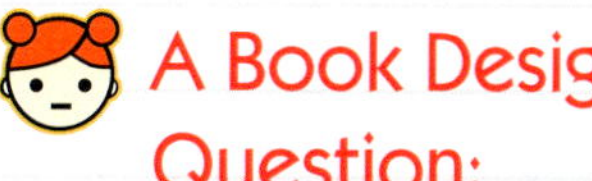

A Book Design Question:
Will you design this book?

Michele's Answer: Yes! I'd love to!

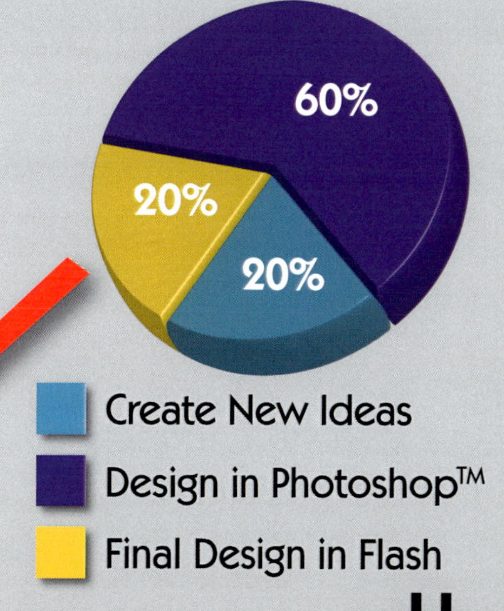

Flash Animation Advertisements

Making a Flash **Advertisement**

A Flash animation advertisement uses a program called Adobe Flash™. Flash can create fast-moving parts and bright, colourful images. These grab and hold our attention while they advertise products and services.

The Flash Software

Flash allows the designer to create and do many amazing things … in seconds. The Flash designer can:

- create moving images
- make them appear and disappear
- make them larger or smaller
- change the colours of images quickly
- add or delete images quickly
- make images "explode" and then come back as a different image … and so much more!

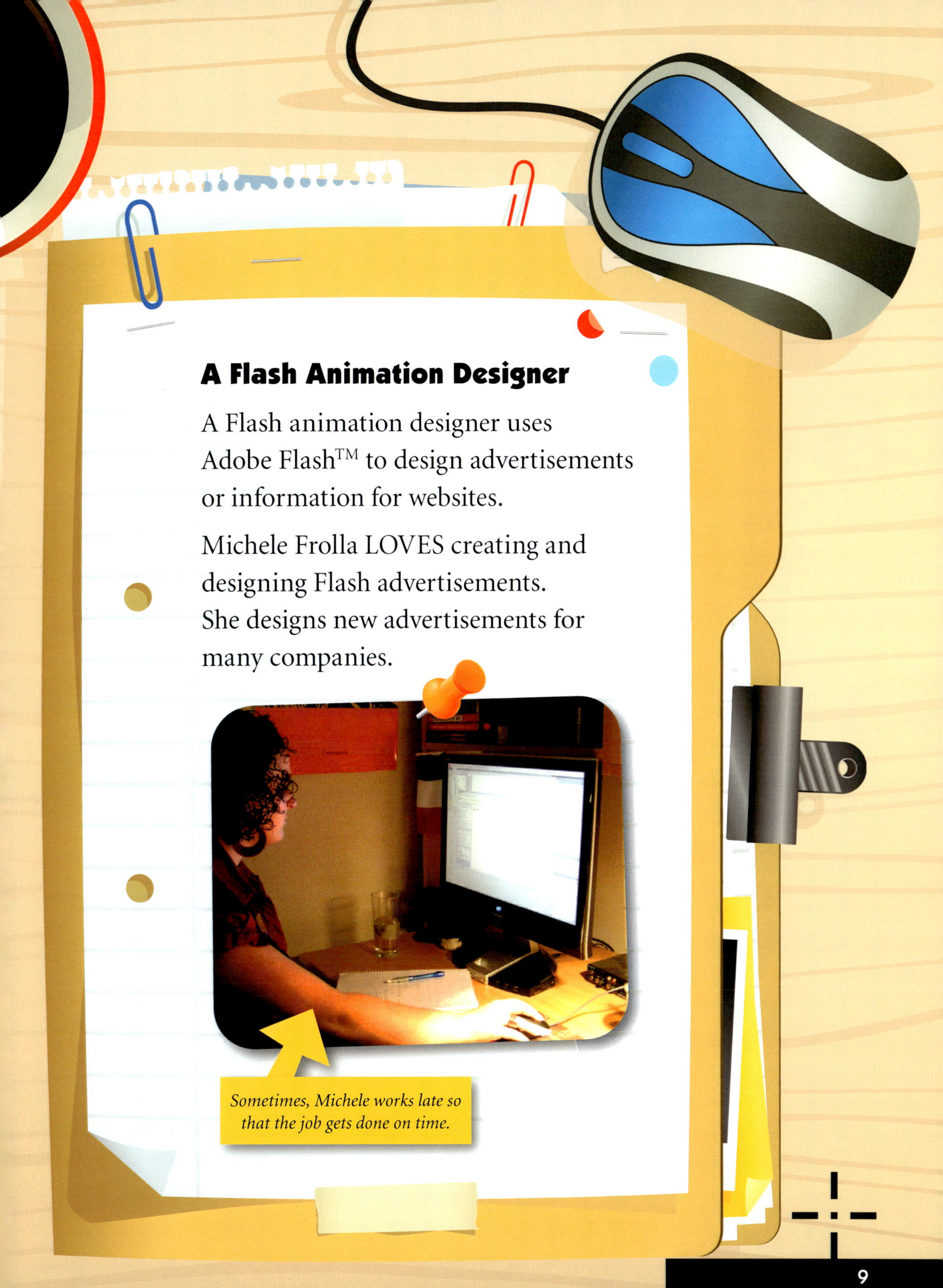

A Flash Animation Designer

A Flash animation designer uses Adobe Flash™ to design advertisements or information for websites.

Michele Frolla LOVES creating and designing Flash advertisements. She designs new advertisements for many companies.

Sometimes, Michele works late so that the job gets done on time.

How Is a Flash Animation **Advertisement** Designed?

1 A Meeting

At the briefing meeting, a car company tells Michele which car will be advertised.

2 The Brief

Michele is given a brief at the meeting. It has information about the car and how they want the ad to "look".

3 The Tag Line

The brief includes the tag line, which describes the car in 3–5 words.

4 Create Ideas

Alone, Michele re-reads the tag line and the brief for the new car. Then Michele:

- writes ideas and key words for the new Flash advertisements
- draws sketches of how the Flash advertisements will look.

5 Brainstorm Ideas

Next, Michele meets with her team of Flash animation designers. They brainstorm and share new ideas. At the end of the meeting, Michele decides which are the best ideas to use.

6 Design the Advertisement

Then Michele uses the best brainstorming ideas to design an advertisement using design software.

7 Ready to Flash Animate

Next, Michele moves her advertisement from the design software into Flash. Now she is ready to animate it using Flash.

8 Design Two Choices

Michele designs two Flash advertisements. The car company can choose the best one.

9 The Staging Site

Finally, Michele posts her two Flash advertisements on the car company's "staging site". The "staging site" is a secure website where the advertisements can be checked by the company.

10 "On the Fly"

Michele phones the car company for an "on the fly" meeting. The comments and questions buzz back and forth, just like a fly!

At the end of this meeting, the car company tells Michele their favourite Flash advertisement.

LOOK AT PAGE 22

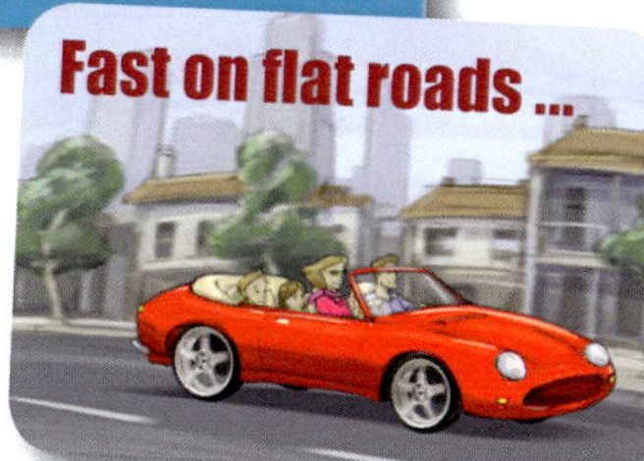

11 Finished!

The advertisement is full of colour and people can see why that car is so good to buy. Now it is ready to be posted on many websites.

Fascinating Flash!

Flash animation is very complex. But many aspects of Flash are fascinating.

Frame and Key Frames

Frames are single pictures or images.

Key frames are like two train stations. Michele decides what action she wants to happen on the way between the two key frames.

TWEENING

In Flash animation, **tweening** is all the action that happens **between** two key frames.

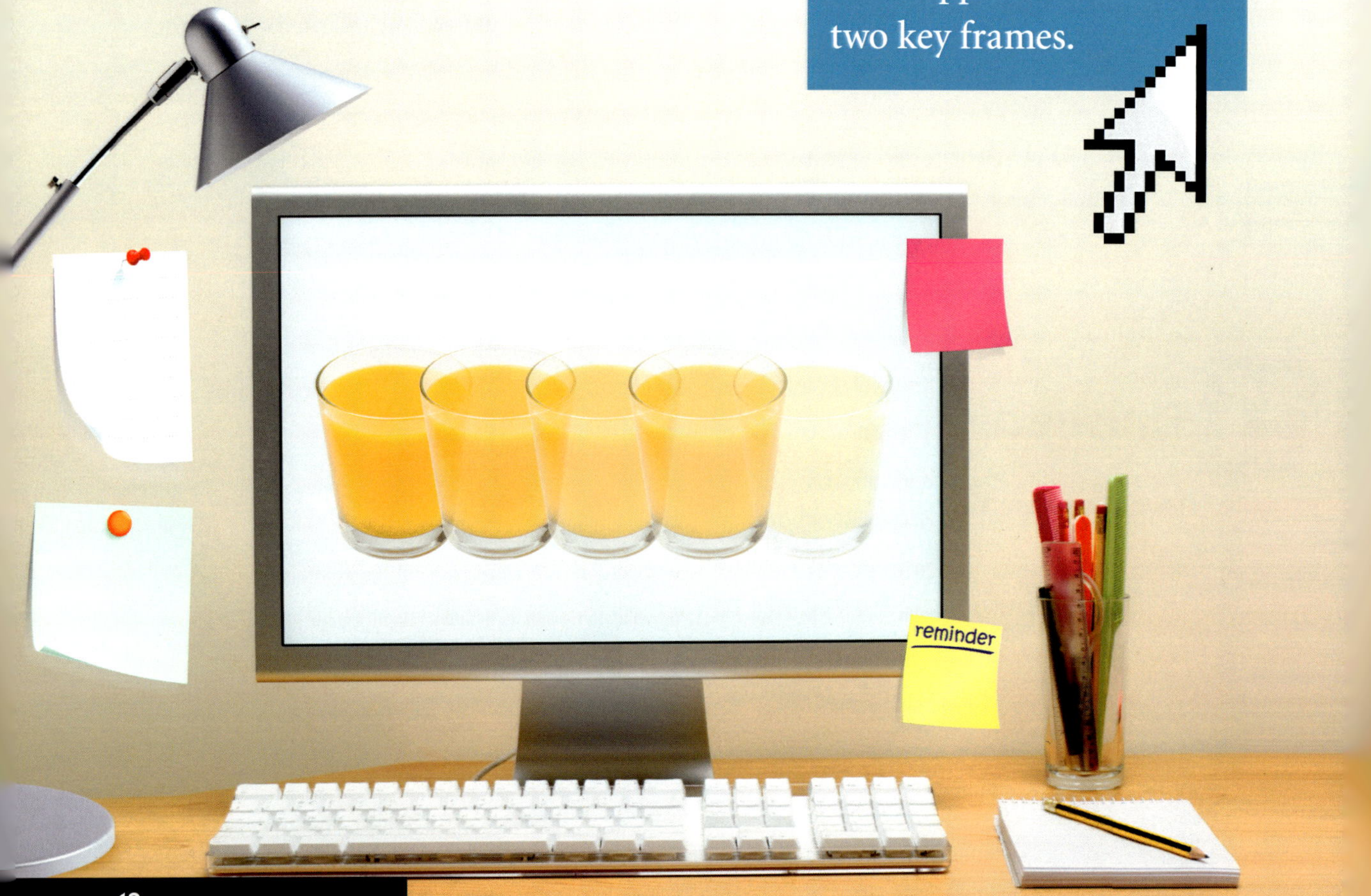

reminder

TIMELINE IN FLASH

The timeline is a panel within Flash that shows all objects that are being animated. Each object appears on its own layer. This is where you control how the object will animate and the length of time it will animate.

This timeline shows how many frames there are for the animator to use to move and fade the glass in the animation.

Key Frame 2

5 10 15 20 25 30

Key Frame 1

the inbetweening

A Tweening Action Between Two Key Frames

Key Frame 1: A glass of orange juice is on the left.

Key Frame 2: It's the same glass of orange juice, but now the glass has moved to the right and faded.

Michele's Job

Michele used Flash to move the glass right and fade out between Key Frame 1 and Key Frame 2.

Key Frame 1

Flash's Job

The Flash program made the images in between Key Frame 1 and Key Frame 2.

OUT

Other **Exciting** Flash **Animations**

Michele can use Flash to create more exciting actions. Her job is to make advertisements so amazing that people will look at them for longer. For example:

Time: Michele can move a glass of juice across the screen for ten seconds.

Words and Objects: Michele can add words to the glass and objects inside the glass.

Fade In and Fade Out: Michele can make a row of apples quickly fade in and then fade out between each key frame.

Colours: Michele can change colours for any part of the tweening action.

Movement: Michele can move a glass of orange juice from one part of an advertisement to another – in a straight line or a wavy line or another shape.

Michele says Flash animation is very exciting. There are so many actions that you can do with Flash. Flash helps her ideas come to life very quickly in new and interesting ways!

Icons in the Toolbox: When Michele creates an animation, there are many tools she needs to use. These are called icons. Below are some of the icons Michele uses the most.

- Select an Object
- Resize an Object
- Type Text
- Select a Colour
- Paintbrush
- Draw a Gradient
- Draw Complex Objects
- Draw a Square
- Draw a Circle

4 Flash Animation Storyboards

Flash **Frame** by **Frame**

A storyboard is like a comic. Words and pictures tell the story. A Flash animation storyboard shows companies how their products will be advertised. It tells, frame by frame, the story from start to finish.

four ice-creams "fan out"

one ice-cream rotates and "fades-in"

FRAME 3

bubblegum burst

"dancing" ice-creams

one ice-cream "scales-up"

FRAME 4

powerful peppermint

FRAME 5

falling ice-creams

5 Are Flash Advertisements Better?

First ... Why **Advertise?**

Why Products Are Advertised

Companies advertise their products or services so people know about them and buy them. Advertisements may also tell people why the product or service is better than other products.

Where Products Are Advertised

Companies can choose many places to advertise:

- newspapers
- magazines
- television
- radio
- billboards
- brochures
- the Internet.

How Advertisements Work

Advertisers use pictures, music and words to persuade people that a product is good. Those who use the product look happier, richer, cleaner, healthier or better in some way. There are many ways advertisements persuade people to buy.

We need a strong "call-to-action".

Where will my customers look?

When Products Are Advertised

Many products are advertised at special times of the year.

Back to School

Products are advertised for school, such as stationery and uniforms.

Valentine's Day

Many products are advertised with red roses or hearts.

Summer

Products are advertised for outdoors, such as sunglasses, sun hats and sunscreen.

Winter

Products are advertised for cold weather such as scarves, thick jackets, heaters and boots.

What Do You Buy?

Before you buy a product such as a bike, read the advertisements and brochures carefully. You can also talk to experts.

Then you can decide if the product is right for you, and for your family's budget.

Flash Animation Is **Best**

TEXT TYPE
Exposition

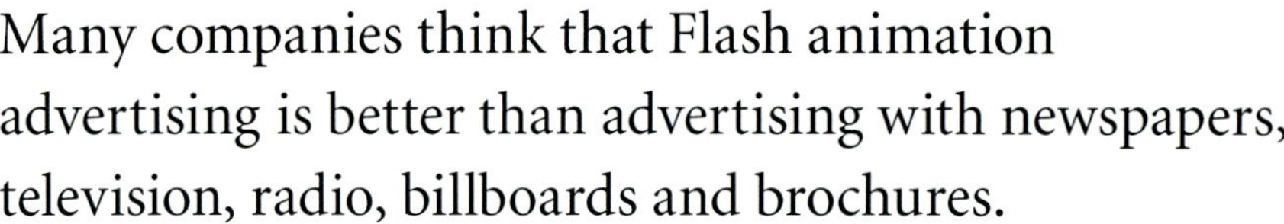

Many companies think that Flash animation advertising is better than advertising with newspapers, television, radio, billboards and brochures.

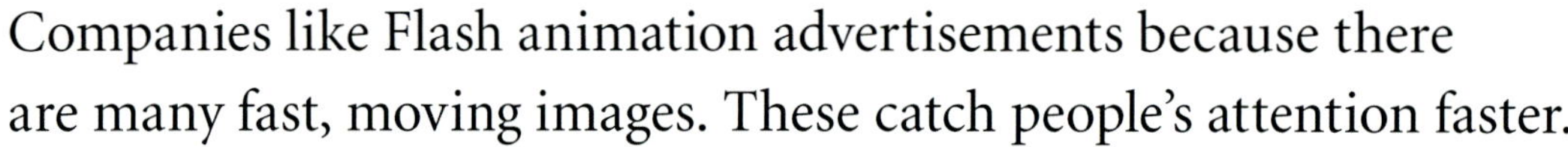

Companies like Flash animation advertisements because there are many fast, moving images. These catch people's attention faster.

Flash animation advertisements can quickly change from a small size to a larger size. People can "mouse-over" the advertisement and make it wider or longer or get more information.

B R I G H T E R

Flash animation advertisements use bright colours and shapes, as well as text. They can change in seconds. It's like magic! The movement and the bright colours may hold our attention for longer than a normal advertisement.

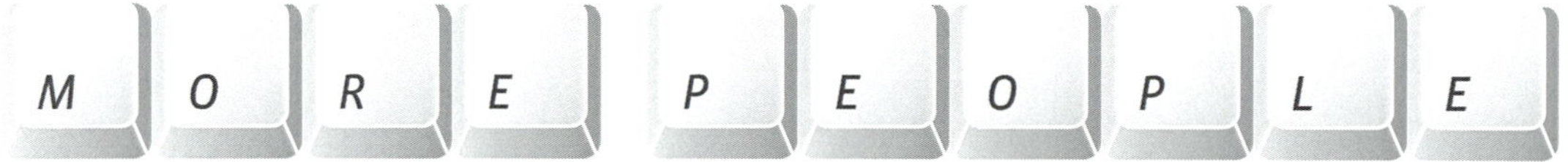

People spend a lot of time on the computer. Flash animation advertising can be used on many websites to get more people's attention.

http://www

Technology

Mouse-Over

"Mouse-over" is when we move our mouse over the Flash animation advertisement or click on it.

CONCLUSION

Companies will keep advertising their products with Flash animation on websites.

This form of advertising provides companies with the best way to reach people. This means that more people may choose to buy their products.

Reviewing the Advertisement

Once the Flash animation advertisements are "live" on websites, people can look at them. Michele Frolla and her team of Flash designers want to know what people think of their advertisements.

A Flash Advertisement

THIS IS A GREAT FLASH ADVERTISEMENT. CLICK ON THE CAR AND A NICE LITTLE POP-UP TELLS YOU HOW THE ADVERTISED CAR IS BETTER THAN OTHER SIMILAR CARS.

THIS ADVERTISEMENT IS SIMPLE, YET EFFECTIVE, AND ATTRACTS YOUNGER BUYERS TO THIS CAR. IT'S ALSO A NICE-LOOKING AD. GIVEN THE COST OF TV ADVERTISING, THIS IS A MUCH CHEAPER OPTION FOR A CAR COMPANY. ”

A MAGAZINE REVIEWER

7 Flash Animation Success

Ads Are Put to the Test

Companies need to find out if their Flash animation advertisements have been a success. They want to know how many people have clicked on their advertisements. The "Click-Through Rate" (CTR) will help them.

Click-Through Rate (CTR)

The CTR is the percentage of clicks on an advertisement divided by the number of times the advertisement appeared on the website. It is then multiplied by 100 to turn it into a percentage. For example:

$$\frac{\text{20 clicks}}{\text{100 advertisements}} \times 100 = \text{20\% CTR}$$

That's an excellent CTR! Every time someone clicks on an advertisement or banner, it is recorded on a computer at a media buying company.

Mathematics

A Media Buying Company

A media buying company buys advertising space on websites for companies that advertise products with Flash.

The media buying company's computer records the "Click-Through Rate" for each Flash advertisement. Then they give the results to the companies.

Index

Glossary

banner	A header or panel on an Internet page that is advertising or promoting something
brainstorm	To have a meeting where everyone comes up with ideas
call-to-action	The part of an advertisement that asks people to do something, like "buy now" or "act quickly"
explode	To burst or split into pieces
gradient	A scale (in this case, of colour) where something goes from strong to weak – for example, dark blue to light blue
Photoshop™	A computer program that lets the user change the way that a photo or image looks
pop-up	A small "window" that pops up on an Internet page
scales up	Increases in size